THE BLABBER REPORT

True Kelley

Dutton Children's Books

The classroom was humming on Monday morning. The mice were finishing up their science posters. Blabber Mouse, who liked to talk and talk, was telling his friends about his weekend . . . in detail.

"I'm sorry to interrupt, Blabber," said Mrs. Numley, the teacher. "But I have an announcement."

The UGLY WORM
nce upon a time...

The End   by Kate

JOAN Presents:
LIFE CYCLE OF AN
AMPHIBEAN

by Jojo

What Came first?
The Frog or the egg?

Butterflies + Worms
Life Stories

by LuLu

by Charlotte
A Tadpole
Grows Up

by Blabber M.

"Class? We will be doing oral book reports next week," she said.

Suddenly, the whole room was dead silent.

For oral book reports, you had to stand up in front of everyone and all their beady little staring eyes. You had to talk about a book for *five* long minutes! Oral book reports were scary!

Five minutes talking was nothing to Blabber. He talked all the time! But an oral report was not like ordinary talking.

"If you all do a good job on your reports, we will have a cheesy-chip cookie party," said Mrs. Numley.

Blabber really wanted to do a good job. If he didn't, no cookies for anyone! The problem was that Blabber's school reports never turned out right.

The too-short
short story!

The too-long
haiku poem!

The colonial times map
that must have fallen in
the toilet.

And today, the science poster.
This time I'll really try, thought Blabber. *I'll try harder than
ever before!*

Everyone was supposed to pick out a book at the library. George loved the book he found called *Snakes!*

JoJo dug out a book called *Root Vegetables.*

Blabber couldn't decide on a book. There were so many!

The next day George wrote out his speech on note cards. Blabber drew snake pictures for him.

Joan was too busy to talk to Blabber. She was reading the encyclopedia, book J-K-L, and putting sticky notes on all the interesting pages.

"Please sit down and do your own work, Blabber," said Mrs. Numley. "Bit by bit and you'll get it done."

At his desk, Blabber doodled on his notebook. He didn't even want to think about his report.

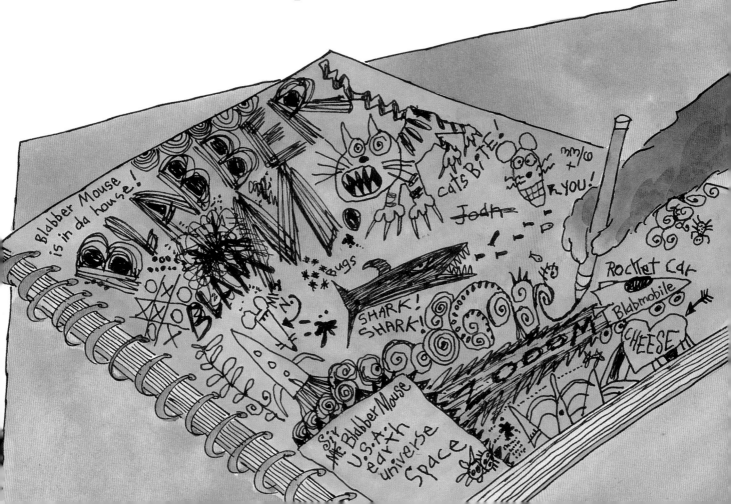

JoJo hated his book.
Boring root vegetables!
Blabber told him a
veggie joke.

Mrs. Numley gave Blabber "The Look." But the joke helped
JoJo plod through the book.

When he got home, JoJo practiced his report in front of the
mirror. He used a lot of paw gestures and facial expressions,
unlike the root veggies he was talking about.

As book report day got closer, Blabber wiggled in his chair even more than usual. He got up to sharpen his pencil thirty-two times. He stared out the window.

At recess, he stared *in* the window. He was too quiet.

"Are you worried about your oral book report?" LuLu asked.

"No prob, Bob! It's a breeze, Louise! No worry-ah, Gloria!" said Blabber. But Blabber was faking it. He was terrified. He was tortured! He hadn't even picked out a book yet!

Oral book report day arrived.

"Who would like to be first?" asked Mrs. Numley.

George said a snake had eaten his note cards! LuLu thought her book might have been stolen by a burglar. Blabber was under his desk with his eyes closed tight. *I am invisible. I am invisible,* he thought.

But Joan wildly waved her paws.

"ME! ME!!!" she yelled.

So Joan was first. She sure was ready! Annoyingly ready. She wore a costume. She had full-color charts. She had handouts. She had cheese samples! It was actually pretty interesting.

"In summary," Joan finished, "I highly recommend the encyclopedia, book J-K-L!"

The class clapped politely, but everyone looked pale and stunned. No one thought they could do as well as that.

"Blabber, you are next," said Mrs. Numley.

Blabber's blood ran cold.

Under his desk, Blabber noticed the book in his backpack, *Scary Dinosaurs.*

Last summer he had read it four times. Perfect!

The mice clapped before Blabber even started. They all fixed their beady little eyes on him. After a dramatic pause, Blabber held up his book and . . .

He froze.
He forgot.
He seized up!

He looked at
the ceiling

and at the floor.

He blinked

and giggled

and
jiggled.

He turned red.

He turned white.

He turned green!

"My . . . my . . . my . . . b-b-book is . . . is . . . is . . . " he
stammered, but he couldn't go on.

"You may sit down, Blabber," said Mrs. Numley.

Blabber slouched back to his seat. His oral book report was a disaster! The whole class thought cookies looked doubtful, but they felt sorry for Blabber and clapped anyway.

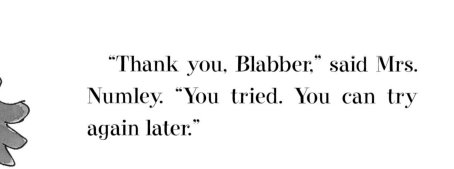

"Thank you, Blabber," said Mrs. Numley. "You tried. You can try again later."

Blabber's heart sank. Later would be even worse! He had let everyone down. And now he hated his favorite book.

George was up next. He forgot what his book was. He stared at his tail. Then he remembered—*Snakcs!*

George read from his note cards. Somehow, he pulled it off and zoomed for the safety of his desk.

In a funny, wobbly voice, JoJo said he did *not* recommend his book *at all.*

LuLu gave her talk and giggled a lot. She had a terrible and fierce fake smile through the whole thing, but she did a pretty good job.

Every day more mice gave their reports.
There were mumblers . . .

and jigglers . . .

and freezers.

Nobody was perfect—except Joan, of course.
Finally Mrs. Numley said, "Good job, everyone.
And Blabber, it's your turn tomorrow." The whole
class looked nervous.

At recess Blabber was not talking and talking. His friends wanted to help. "Just do your report bit by bit," said JoJo. "And try practicing in front of a mirror tonight. It worked for me."

"Use these sticky notes," Joan suggested.

"Props are good," said LuLu. She drew a picture for him to use.

George helped Blabber make notes on note cards. Blabber thought they might actually work.

Bit by bit Blabber felt better about his report. He practiced in front of his mirror.

He marked interesting facts in his book with sticky notes. He had LuLu's picture. And best of all, he had a set of note cards that told him exactly what to say.

The next morning, Mrs. Nunney asked, "Are you ready to give your report, Blabber?"

"Yes," said Blabber.

He stood up in front
of the room and waited
for the class to calm down.

Suddenly, he felt sick! Where were his note cards? He had left them on the bus! He couldn't think of a single thing to say! What was his book about? What *was* his book?

All the beady little eyes were on him. Staring.
Scary . . . thought Blabber.

"SCARY DINOSAURS!" he yelled.
"YES!" cried the class.

Then they all helped Blabber get through it.

Before Blabber knew it, he was done.
"And that's the Blabber Report!" he said.

Everyone was cheering!

"Super report!" said Mrs. Numley.
"Thank you," said Blabber. "I couldn't
have done it without such a great
audience!"

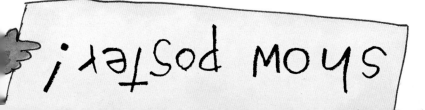

DUTTON CHILDREN'S BOOKS
A division of Penguin Young Readers Group

Published by the Penguin Group
Penguin Group (USA) Inc., 375 Hudson Street, New York, New York 10014, U.S.A.
Penguin Group (Canada), 90 Eglinton Avenue East, Suite 700, Toronto, Ontario,
Canada M4P 2Y3 (a division of Pearson Penguin Canada Inc.) • Penguin Books Ltd.
80 Strand, London WC2R ORL, England • Penguin Ireland, 25 St Stephen's Green,
Dublin 2, Ireland (a division of Penguin Books Ltd) • Penguin Group (Australia),
250 Camberwell Road, Camberwell, Victoria 3124, Australia (a division of Pearson
Australia Group Pty Ltd) • Penguin Books India Pvt Ltd, 11 Community Centre,
Panchsheel Park, New Delhi - 110 017, India • Penguin Group (NZ), Cnr Airborne
and Rosedale Roads, Albany, Auckland 1310, New Zealand (a division of Pearson
New Zealand Ltd) • Penguin Books (South Africa) (Pty) Ltd, 24 Sturdee Avenue,
Rosebank, Johannesburg 2196, South Africa • Penguin Books Ltd, Registered
Offices: 80 Strand, London WC2R ORL, England

CIP Data is available.

Published in the United States by Dutton Children's Books,
a division of Penguin Young Readers Group
345 Hudson Street, New York, New York 10014
www.penguin.com/youngreaders

Manufactured in China • First Edition
ISBN 978-0-525-47809-6
10 9 8 7 6 5 4 3 2 1

For Torlis

With thanks again to
Debbie Cantrell